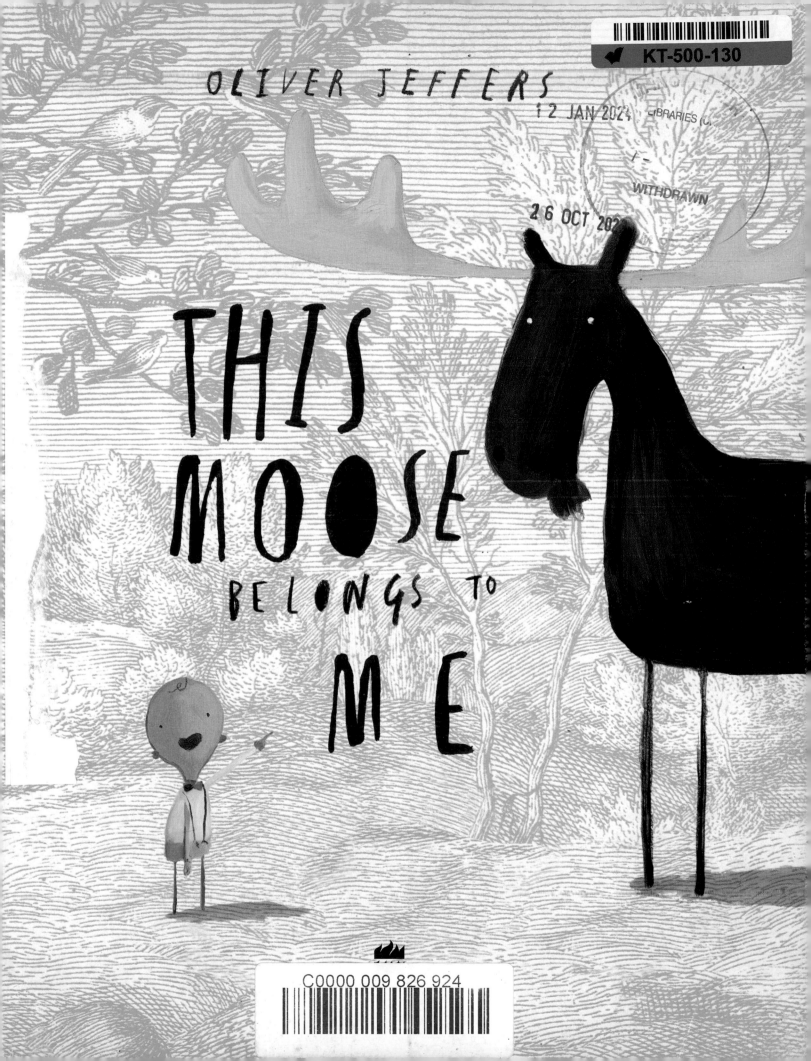

OLIVER JEFFERS

THIS MOOSE BELONGS TO ME

For
MAC and ADRianna

First published in hardback in Great Britain by HarperCollins Children's Books in 2012
First published in paperback in 2013

10 9 8 7 6 5 4 3 2 1

ISBN: 978-0-00-726390-5

Text and illustrations copyright © Oliver Jeffers 2012

Additional landscape backgrounds reprinted by kind permission of the Estate of Alexander Dzigurski, copyright © Alexander Dzigurski:
Majestic Tetons 1963; *Morning Light, Carmel Valley* 1988; *Jenny Lake* 1983; *Grand Teton Vista* 1984; *Mt Hood, Oregon* 1972;
Santa Cruz Ice Plant 1989; *Jackson Lake, Wyoming* 1978

HarperCollins Children's Books is a division of HarperCollins Publishers Ltd.

The author/illustrator asserts the moral right to be identified as the author/illustrator of the work.

Visit our website at: www.harpercollins.co.uk

Printed and bound in China

Wilfred owned a moose.

He hadn't always owned a moose.
The moose came to him a while
ago and he knew, just KNEW,
that it was meant to be his.

He thought he
would call him
Marcel.

He began following Marcel,
explaining the rules of how
to be a good pet.

Much of the time, it seemed as though the moose wasn't listening, but Wilfred knew he was. Mostly because he followed RULE 4 very well:

NOT making too much NOISE while Wilfred plays his RECORD collection.

Sometimes the moose wasn't a very good pet.
He generally ignored Rule 7: going
whichever way Wilfred wants to go.

The moose had a very good sense
of direction, and Wilfred did not. And
because the moose was particularly
poor on Rule 7 [subsection b]:
MAINtAining a certain
proximity to home, Wilfred
quickly learned to bring some string
along on their outings so he could
find his way back again.

Sometimes the moose was
an excellent pet. He had
no trouble with RULE 11:
providing shelter
from the RAIN.

or Rule 16: Knocking down things that are out of WILFRED's reach.

One day, as Wilfred discussed their plans for
the coming year on a particularly long walk,
he made a terrible discovery...

Someone else thought they owned the moose.

Wilfred was dumbstruck.
This moose was Marcel, not Rodrigo.
The old lady was mistaken and
Wilfred thought it only proper
that he correct her.

This MOOSE Belongs to ME! he explained.

And to prove it, he called Marcel.

But the moose did not respond.
He seemed more interested in
the old lady.

good Rodrigo.

Embarrassed and enraged,
Wilfred rushed off for home.

But in his haste, and
miles from anywhere,
he tripped over his string
and got tangled up.

And there he lay.

Wilfred was beginning to get a little bit worried.
It was past his home time now, and the
monsters would be out soon.

He had just
ruled out the last
of his options...

when along came the moose...

...and performed **RULE 73** brilliantly:

Rescuing your owner from
PERILOUS SITUATIONS.

All was forgiven.
And perhaps, Wilfred admitted,
he'd never really owned the
moose anyway.

With that in mind, he and the moose reached a compromise. The moose would agree to all of Wilfred's rules…

...whenever it suited him.